Kittrell J Warren

Ups and Downs of Wife Hunting

Merry Jokes for Camp Perusal

Kittrell J Warren

Ups and Downs of Wife Hunting
Merry Jokes for Camp Perusal

ISBN/EAN: 9783337379919

Printed in Europe, USA, Canada, Australia, Japan

Cover: Foto ©Andreas Hilbeck / pixelio.de

More available books at **www.hansebooks.com**

UPS AND DOWNS

OF

WIFE HUNTING:

OR,

MERRY JOKES FOR CAMP PERUSAL.

BY

A PRIVATE of COMPANY B., 11th Reg't Ga. Vol's.

———— ••• ————

SECOND EDITION.

———— ••• ————

AUGUSTA, GA.:
PRINTED AT THE OFFICE OF THE CONSTITUTIONALIST.

———

1861.

TO

The Army of the Potomac,

WITH THE BEST AFFECTIONS OF THE AUTHOR,

THIS LITTLE BOOK

IS

RESPECTFULLY DEDICATED.

WIFE HUNTING.

CHAPTER FIRST.

The Author explains what is not his object in writing—gives his opinion of the women, and concludes with a hint as to what his object is.

It may be supposed, from the title of my pamphlet, that I am venting a settled grudge against the women—assigning them a position among the "trifles, light as air," or, at least, arraying myself in an attitude of hostility to the sex. Such a suspicion I disavow *toto cœlo et ab imo pectoro*. I have loved them from my youth up) and they will forever continue to be a staple commodity in the market of my affections. Although, through many long weary years they have persistently nettled me with the whips and arrows of outrageous fortune ; although they have presented me slippers sufficient in point of quantity to start a large wholesale shoe-store, (with numbers ranging from one to ten) ; although they have reduced and lacerated my poor heart until it will scarcely rival in dimensions a common-sized chew of tobacco ; although they have done "all this and more," yet, "with all their faults, I love them still."

Some, again, may pay me the compliment to suppose that the object of these presents is the presentation of a series of imaginary incidents, containing a "good moral." This is a usual subterfuge with writers whose works possess no intrinsic points of attraction. Indeed, so many love stories, novels and tales in general, are seasoned with a "good moral," that the good morals of the community are suffering

considerable depletion.   I disavow any such design; nor do
I propose to bestow a blessing upon "fallen humanity," to
kindle the genial fires of hope upon the hearth-stone of a
freezing heart, nor do any ether hifalutin' or catch-penny
act, as an introduction of this little scrap of a pamphlet. My
purpose, and my only purpose, is to give a sort of " Thirty
Years' View " of the trials I have passed through, the both-
erations I have undergone, and the martyrdom I have en-
dured, in searching for a wife ; to present a summary review
of " The Sorrows of a Poor Old Man " who has boxed every
point of the matrimonial compass, and yet remains, and is
likely to continue, *sans uxorem.*

" With this declaration on my part," oh, reader, " are you
still willing to proceed ?"

CHAPTER SECOND.

The Author introduces himself to the public in a modest and becoming manner.

My father, Mr. Gersham Huggins, lived in the County of
Wilkes, and State of Georgia, at the period of my nativity,
which important event occurred on the 15th day of October,
in the year of Grace one thousand eight hundred and fourteen.   During my infancy, he (being a man of strong attach-
ments and great peculiarities) determined to name me after
a faithful ox then recently deceased, from which circumstance I have ever since rejoiced in the euphonious name of
Jezebel Huggins.   At the age of fourteen, I was sent to
Athens, where I entered the preparatory department of
Franklin College, then under the supervision of Dr. Church,
who was a real " Church Militant " to all idle school boys.
I was then the only surviving member of my father's
family, and he determined to expend his scanty means in
my education,

About three months after I arrived at Athens, my father
died, leaving my uncle Timothy his executor, with instructions to pay all his honest debts, (and he didn't owe any

dishonest ones,) and to keep me at school until the overplus was exhausted.

Uncle Tim, who was a plain, blunt, illiterate, solid, substantial sort of a man, considered this disposition of my meagre patrimony so unwise and injudicious, that he actually believed my father was " beyant hisself " when he made it ; but this fact he couldn't prove, and the testamentary edict being unmistakable, I remained at Franklin until I had waded through the eight hundred and seventeen dollars and eleven cents, which composed the paternal leavings.

Uncle Tim was several years older than pappy, and his children having all married off, I soon became quite a pet and favorite with him and Aunt Jerushy. He, however, sometimes grew crusty and severe, and occasionally even boisterous, turbulent and terrible ; for, with all his goodness, sincerity and kindness, he knew nothing about how to be gentle and mild. I spent the winter vacations at his house, and during the balance of the year (as he couldn't read without spelling, and of course wrote)still more indifferently) we held but little correspondence.

Under such auspices, oh, reader, I grew to be a man, such as I am. And here I will insert a word as to my appearance and proportions, physically and physiognomically : " I was not formed for sportive tricks, to court an amorous looking-glass," though I might as well have been courting looking-glasses as women, for the benefit I have derived from it. It seems that Dame Nature, in assorting the ingredients with which to set me up, made up her mind to do her "level prettiest " to construct a queer and hard-looking specimen of masculinity. In that effort she didn't bungle : I am five feet nine in my stockings, (or anybody else's,) have black hair, heavy red whiskers, squint pop eyes, sharp cheek bones, one club foot, and a nose which describes the arc of parabola. If you desire a more minute description of my *personelle*, I am pained to say, Ladies, that the facilities at my command are not sufficient to furnish it ; anon, I hope to be able to give you a *vis-a-vis* prospect of my tangible individuality.

Wisdom's Retreat, Starkville, April 21st, 1861.

CHAPTER THIRD.

It is a well-established fact, that the residue of animated nature is a counterpart and imperfect type of our race. The politician is mirrored in the craftiness and cunning of the fox ; the statesman in the sagacity and dignity of the elephant ; the secret foe in the serpentinity of the serpent ; the bowing and scraping dandy in the head-bobbing performances of the Muscovy duck, and that exquisite model of feminine perfection, the Coquette, is aptly miniatured by the wary, graceful and dignified insect which bears the title of " spider." But to amplify : The spider spreads his web in convenient proximity to some secure hiding-place, whither he repairs, practically saying, by his ensconcement; " There is no spider in these parts." In due time, an incautious fly " gets his foot into it," and flutters manfully, (or flyfully,) but in vain, to extricate himself. Mons. Spider struts pompously from his retirement, halts at the apex of his hole, hoists himself upon his locomotive props, and gives a stare of innocent amazement, as though he were really at a loss to determine the cause of so much noise and confusion in and about his premises ; holds one ear down to be certain of the intruder's identity, and then charges, captures, and bears his victim away ; after which, he resolves himself into a " Committee of the *Hole* on the State of the Fly," and resolves unanimously that the latter be " chawed,"

Now, before I proceed to draw the parallel, I wish to direct attention to the fact, that I do not asperse the motives or conduct of the spider. He (like her ladyship) is a professional sharper, and must of necessity let all the ends he aims at be to rope in suckers.

Ah, reader, when J. found myself accidentally writing the word "sucker," it touched the sensitive nerve of my feelings, and battered violently against the flood-gates of my eyes. Like the " Ancient Mariner," I must not, will not, proceed, until I empty into your sympathetic bosom a recollection which that word (acting as Memory's express agent) brings to me :

My grandfather, you remember, was the officer in command at the battle of Hog Pens; the enemy had become too numerous and fearful for his exhausted soldiers to withstand them. Long and desperately did they struggle, hourly expecting the arrival of reinforcements. Often and anxiously did they strain their vision to catch a glimpse of the recruits, until, at length, they could stand it no longer, and demanded a cessation of hostilities, in tones vibrating the music of a threatened mutiny. "Look once more," said my grandfather to his lieutenant, "and see if no *succor* is approaching." Having obeyed instructions, the officer dolorously replied, "nary succor." Whereupon, my chivalrous progenitor and his redoubtable subaltern, finding they could not beat the enemy, beat a retreat—beat it considerably. The kind old soul has long since "passed the buck" of his virtues and frailties to a degenerate posterity; but I shall never forget how he used to weep at the recital of this simple but thrilling event. It was his custom, when oppressed by sorrow, to wring—not his hand, but—his nose—and through the vista of intervening years he is still visible to the eye of Memory—telling my father of this circumstance, and pulling his (my grandfather's, not my father's) nose, as if it were a pump, to pump up the tears which flowed at such times. Peace to my grandfather's ashes, from which the lie (ley) has been thoroughly extracted !

Well, now, I too have wandered off, until I find myself in the position, and typified by the conduct of a certain member of the brute family, which, when pursuing the fresh spoor of a receding deer, suddenly breaks off to a terrible tangent in the "wild hunt" after a rabbit. To return—not from the rabbit, but the digression :

Her ladyship spreads the net-work of her charms, and then "spreads herself" to render them available; drafts recruits from Webster's Unabridged and Moore's Melodies to defend her professions of earnestness, candor and sincerity ; and by her sanctity and seriousness, plainly as her positive declarations *would say*, says, "There is no coquette just here."

At last, Mr. Ichabod Spindle (if you please) is caught in
the web; his sighs, heart-flutterings and other takings on
(for when a fellow's taken in he always takes on) cause her
to advance. " Oh, dear, she is so surprised, flattered and
complimented that Mr. Spindle should see anything in her
(poor modest soul) to admire !"—watches to find out if he
is really a victim, and having satisfied herself on that point,
as certainly as the spider raises his subdued and powerless
fly, does she lift the stultified and unresisting Ichabod, who
becomes, (figuratively, but not less forcibly,) a veritable
chawec. I have had considerable acquaintance, and some
experience with this amiable and interesting species of the
Genus mulieries To one of them I owe a debt of gratitude.
which, like the balance of my debts, I am not now prepared
to cash ; for when I was a bashful, retiring young gawk, she
tamed me, rendered me bridle-wise, (to use a figure,] and
furnished my face with a Fort Sumter fortification of brass,
behind which the modesty of your humble servant has ever
since remained securely protected from all assaults. Yes,
my dear, good-hearted reader, her conduct was so benificent,
that I was never afterwards compelled to resort to the course
pursued by David, indicated by the head note to the
seventy-seventh Psalm. With her I entered the novitiate
of my "Ups and Downs." She put me ,through a course
of sprouts; [calcitraciously speaking,] to the which I have
since become *amanzingly* and *stupendously* accustomed.

But I will reserve the particulars of that adventure for
the next chapter: promising, however, that the circumstances therein related occurred in the summer of '32, [the
last year I remained at school,] and while yet I was on the
cradle side of my eighteenth birth-day.

CHAPTER FOURTH.

The Author waxes lucky—swims in a sea of glory, and gets a ducking.

About one mile from Athens, in those days, stood the residence of Mr. John Philpot, or *alias* Goodlesberry, whose daughter "I meet by chance" for the first time among a collection of young people assembled at my boarding-house, on the fourth day of July. Now, as I had not before ventured to go into a crowd of strange young ladies, and particularly as I had never yet embarked in the perilous enterprise of chatting familiarly with one I had not previous ly seen, my conduct on this occasion was indeed strange. But so it happened; I actually came in, received an intro-duction, sat down by Miss Ellen and commenced a conver-sation. She was a month younger than myself, but many years my senior in a knowledge of the world, and the accessible avenues to the human heart. She saw I was a fit subject, and determined to have with me an "immediate and unconditional" *affaire de ceur.* From that time I was a "goner." In less than one short hour I was, *prehaps*, the worst duped individual that has existed since the days of Theseus. The evening passed away and we separated; but from that time I could not eat, drink, dream, meditate nor do anything else unmixed with thoughts of dear, delightful, saccharine Ellen. Her voice mingled in every murmur of the brooklet; here eye sparkled in every pearly dew-drop, and her ottar of-roses smell I snuffed in every whiff of the "tainted breeze." She was a compended, condensed and collated digest of all the elements in the integration of per-fect loveliness—a machine invented for the express purpose of manufacturing the most exquisite heart emotions—a monstrosity—an awfality—in short, a real "whopper." Oh, how anxiously I yearned, how honestly I labored, to be like her in every respect. Sometimes I would congratulate my-self that I had let off some sentence with her peculiar vocal modulations; and not unfrequently did I feel exultant at the thought that I had charmed an associate with a *fac simile* of her fascinating smiles. The reader must here be informed that I had not become (at the period referred to) intimately acquainted with my own personal appearance. Aunt Jerushy had often told me I was a "purty boy," and I had too much affection for her, too much confidence in her taste and veracity, and decidedly too much veneration for her age, to suffer the testimony of a looking-glass to weigh in the balance against her deliberately-formed opinion; besides, "love," you remember, "hides a multitude of faults;" and as I am on remarkably intimate terms with myself, Love, of course, concealed my countenancial misfortunes. Love undoubtedly had its hands full. I have intimated that I *fell* in love with Miss Ellen; and I take this early occasion to correct that statement. "Fell" is too passive a word to express the luxury of my emotions. I jumped—I pitched—as "the unthinking horse rusheth into the battle," I rushed into a love scrape with her. Three times a week did I repair to the Goodlesberry Mecca, and as often was my devotion intensified by the pilgrimage; for Ellen told me, by a thousand *modest* signs and tokens, that life was "dark and dreary" without me. I resolved, of course, to marry her. She, as well as myself, was not likely to be troubled with much of the stuff that money's made of, but I didn't care a fig for that. I loved her, and that was enough to fix my resolution: for, calculating consequences is a species of mathematics I was never much addicted to figuring at. Where we would live, or what we would feed on, were matters too commonplace and corn-bread-i-fied to claim much of my attention. I sat down to write to my uncle, informing him of my intended nuptials. I felt that I ought to write a letter commensurate with the importance of the subject under consideration, and to the accomplishment of that object I marshalled my energics. My mind was in those days a cross between dignity and clownishness, pedantry and drollery. Which of these mental characteristics had the upper hand in the document then constructed, I leave the reader to determine, after a careful perusal. But I must state, as a sort of preface to the letter, that those who were acquainted with me in my boyhood—and their name is legion (perhaps I should have said the Messrs. Legion)—will readily certify, from its characteristic style, that it is a genuine and authentic document, as it really is. It ran thus :

My Dear Sir and Uncle :

I deem it an imperative duty to apprise you, without deferring, but with great deference, of the illimitably important consummation about to be most devoutly perpetrated. I am now upon the giddy verge of committing connubiation. I am about to pluck from its parent stem one of the loveliest flowers that ever bloomed in pristine gorgeousness outside of the garden of Paradise. Yes, my cherished, venerated and antique relative, I am about to effect a unition consonant with the promptings of a pre-existent adoration. A very Ganymede, my fidelity shall remain unabated until the lamp of life wavers in feebly-flickering corruseations, preliminary to its extinguishment. We will embark on the voyage of life with no freight but the cargo of reciprocal affection, for my cynosure is deficient in pecuniary resources. But I should contemn myself were I mercenary. No! no! I believe you will agree with me, that pure, exalted love is an antidote for poverty, and, indeed, for "all the ills that flesh is heir to." I trust the design I have thus marked out on life's trestle-board will receive your ungrudging approbation. To you is yet intrusted the argosy of my incipient independence, but my heart has no legal custodian, and I haven't a suspicion that you will endeavor or even desire to thwart its purposes or "fetter its steps of freedom." With much love to you and Aunt Jerushy—with unfeigned anxiety for your continued conjugal felicity, and an earnest solicitation for an immediate response, I am, my dear sir, your humble servant and very affectionate friend and nephew,

JEZEBEL HUGGINS.

July 15th, 1832.

For a moment I hesitated about sending a letter so unintelligible to the *sendee*, but not doubting that it would inspire a feeling of awe in the mind of my "antique relations," and secure their support in all my future measures, I mailed it, and it went safely, and was received in due time. My uncle opened it and surveyed it with all the symptoms of a tertiary stage of surprise. He attempted to read it, turned it over to Aunt Jerushy, who (contrary to her usual custom) didn't even venture an opinion as to its meaning. It was next handed to the neighbors, and finally lodged in the hands of Sir Oracle, the settlement school-teacher, who turned out school for three whole days to translate it, and rode seventeen miles after a big dictionary to aid in his "literary researches" thus planned out. I since learned from contemporaneous authority, that on Saturday evening, the 29th of July, 1832, at 31 minutes after five, he finished this Herculean job, and "rested from his labors." His translation ran thus: "He's a gwine two marry; wants yore advise; the woman he's gwine for two marry is named Miss Ganny Mede; don't keer so monstrous much about pecuniary money matters; thinks he loves Ganny, (euros name,) and 'lows love'l do 'thout any vittels; sends love two you and misses huggings, and wants you two rite two him a mediately."

No letter could have more successfully coppered on my uncle's feelings than this; and it's strange I didn't know it would. He and Aunt Jerushy had lived as orderly and peaceably as any other "two couples" in Christendom, but he had never, during a thirty years' acquaintance, told her a word about love; and I afterwards had occasion to learn that there was no class of community for which he conceived such unutterable detestation, as those drones who regard not the necessities of the morrow. The answer, then, of Paul to Festus would not have been appropriate on this occasion, for my uncle *was mad.* His contempt for me, for my intentions and my pedantry—and he had never seen anything of that sort before—knew no bounds. In vain did Aunt Jerushy—

My good old aunty,
Kind, accommodating aunty—

as she sat with her elbows on her knees, cradling her jaws in the palms of her hands, and smoking her pipe, upside down; in vain did she endeavor to palliate the unpardonableness (if you can say unpardonableness the first trial you ain't drunk) of my offense: " Now, may be," she remarked, "that young uman's put a spell on him; or belikes he's got a spell of the longivity, ur some sich. Lawzy me; I remember when Jemimy Ann Stringer put a spell on Mr. Wilkins' son Bob, and he run on a mity site of sich. I lay that's what Jezzy's got." To these charitable suggestions, my uncle (who was just then letting off steam in a letter to me) made no reply, and was in no wise affected by them, excepting as they unconsciously crept into his cranium and produced a confusion of his ideas, and consequently rendered his letter a medley as unintelligible, in some respects, as my own. Now, my uncle was no "repeater" in writing; he didn't put his hand to the pen and look back; but having finished writing, he folded, sealed and mailed the manuscript without more ado. His reply, therefore, told me substantially, that I was a fool: that I was a sweet piece to be talking about marrying; that I'd better wait "outwell" the rings made by my baby garters had "growed outen my lugs;" said the spell put on Bob Wilkins was a spell of the simples; said Bob was a "harrydick" from the religion of his fathers, (had joined the temperance society,) and wan't no "patternt to go by;" threatened to give me a double dose of the spell and longivities; reminded me again that I was a fool; considered me a "hunnyfied mess;" thought my senses were "upsot;" asked me what I'd feed on "ef I didn't hav no vittels:" repeated the statement that I was a fool; surmised I thought I was "mity smart;" "'speeted" I'd "git to the Assalum yit, ef I kep' on improvin';" taunted me with not caring anything for money; didn't reckon I'd ever have any great quantity to care about, the way I was going on; said the "gal was jist a projicin', and ment to make a fool outen me; and closed his letter by shrewdly observing that I was "a triflin', no 'count, good-for-nothin' fool."

This letter reached me, (as bad luck would have it,) or rather I reached it, (for I came home and found it on my table,) about a half hour after Miss Ellen had presented me my ambulatory credentials, *alias* walking-papers. Yes, sympathizing reader, she had disposed of me in a manner I did not expect. I was so confident she would marry me, that when I asked her, and she said "No," I thought she certainly didn't understand the question; and so I asked her again, and again she told me "No," without even deigning to offer the usual excuses, apologies and regrets I have since heard so often repeated. In other words, she was tired of me! With a heart as heavy as loadstone, and a brain as hot

as Vesuvius was (when she raised a row with her neighbors—Herculaneum and Pompeii—because they wouldn't
"lie furder,") I sought my room, found and opened Uncle
Tim's letter. I hoped to get relief there. I got it—in a
horn. When I saw how correctly he had predicted my fate,
how little he regarded my fine feelings, and the contempt
my pedantry had engendered in his mind, I felt like bursting into—not tears; they are species of *draughts* seldom
drawn at the instance of anything affecting the status of my
inner self—I felt like bursting into----well----I felt like bursting into a fit of *Bombastes Furioso*-ism! Were I to give
a full description of my feelings at that moment, before the
task could be completed, the English language would be
reduced to the cadaverousness of a Job's turkey. I " sat
down and pouted" and laughed alternately, until at length
my guardian muse softly breathed into my ears the plaintive words—" Hoss, poetize!" Whereupon, I slung my fin-
gers across my quill, which cantered off the following lines :

> Oh! Ellen is a curious creature,
> As strange in ways as fair in feature;
> I wish I was a Baptist Preacher,
> There are some things I'd like to teach her.

> I'd tell her, yes, I'd surely tell her
> She oughtn't so to treat a feller;
> Her little foot with shoe so yeller
> Wan't made to use as a propeller.

[The yellow shoe here referred to was not a fact, but a
fiction, warranted by poetic lie-sense.]

> I'd tell her the way that she's a doing
> Will be a many a feller's ruin-g;
> That to those who for her hand are suing,
> Trouble will be always brewing.

At this point I lost my mental reckoning, and began a
series of the most interesting dreams that ever flitted before
the slumbering faculties of a mortal. My nuptial night had
arrived, and Ellen and I were really in *articulo matrimonii;*
I thought my uncle and aunt were there, willing witnesses,
and happy at the anticipated consummation. The former
was elegantly rigged off in a suit of court livery, balancing
himself in the rear of a big six cigar, and occasionally nudg-
ing the tips of his pump-soled boots with a nice little rattan

which he held in his hand. Aunt Jerushy was dressed in Brussels silk; her head decorated with a thousand fluttering parti-colored ribbons ; her pipe, spectacles and old fashioned manners all ignored and repudiated, presenting in her furrowed and time-worn form so gaudily arrayed, a painful type of the "whited sepulchres." I thought my uncle and aunt were billing and cooing in the most morbidly love-sick manner. The scene changed : The crowd had gone ; Ellen and I were in the parlor alone ; I embraced the occasion to give vent to my overflowing emotions, (from my childhood I have been an audible dreamer.) "Delectable angel," said I, "charming, egregious and most remarkable female, my 'whole undivided' heart, from 'centre to circumference' is yours ; not 'yours in haste,' but yours forever ; not 'yours respectfully,' but yours without respect 'to consequences. This hand, on which I now propose to imprint the nuptial kiss is mine, 'individually and collectively,' mine 'in the abstract, and mine in the concrete.'" With this, I now imprinted the imaginary kiss, when loud peals of laughter awoke me. A number of my school-fellows had come into the room, had read my effusion, heard my enthusiastic remarks, and seen me kiss the inkstand in a "violent and tumultuous" manner, which, in return, kindly discharged its contents over the front part of my new suit. Now, to have revealed what I most anxiously desired to keep secret, and to have rendered myself the target of noisy burlesque, were certainly distressing visitations of Fate ; but, in addition to these calamities, to have had my only decent clothes, the last suit I was entitled to from my exhausted patrimony, so stained and blackened as to render them unfit for effectual service, was indeed a draught of the dregs of bitterness. On the next day I made a solemn vow never again to be found in the company of a single woman, unless unavoidably driven thither, and to court no more forever—a vow which I reduced to writing, and have ever since kept—in my trunk.

CHAPTER FIFTH.

The Author performs an interesting occular gyration.

I worked on the ink splotches until I got them sufficiently erased to present a pretty fair burlesque imitation of Joseph's coat of many colors, and once more hopped up in the world of gallantry. My principal object now was to spite my uncle, Miss Ellen and the rest of the world, by marrying immediately, and that without reference to affections, circumstances or anything else. Thus determined, I began to pay my respects to Misses Elfrina and Elbrida Bell, two clever, buxom, illiterate lasses, for whom I had about as much love as a frog has for mint juleps. I couldn't manage to scatter these sweet creatures, but, nevertheless, on my third visit, without giving her any premonitory indications, I endeavored to guage my voice so that the elder would not understand me, and popped the question to the younger sister. The dear creature bore this unexpected attack upon the fortress of her affections with remarkable courage, fortitude and presence of mind, and actually answered "Yes," before my tongue had lolled back in its place, after firing the before-mentioned verbal discharge. But here I found myself in a scrape. In my excitement I had spoken louder than I had intended to, and both had heard me. I had not designated by name the individual I was addressing, and being squint-eyed, one eye was aimed (as though it would go off) in the direction of each of the damsels ; each, therefore, considered herself courted, and both blushed, hung their heads and answered "Yes." This was a scrape I hadn't bargained fer ; to be in the incipient stages of Mormonism so early in life, was embarrassing. I hadn't the spunk to talk out of it, so I went home, wrote a letter to the older sister, explaining, apologizing, and using all the means at my command to relieve the awkwardness of her situation. But my excitement had not yet worn off—my note was addressed and directed to Miss E. Bell, a name applicable alike to each. This caused another "fuss in the family," and I received, in reply, a verbal message to repair thither immediately. I have not yet obeyed that summons.

Whether, during the intervening thirty years, the Misses Bell have all the while sat primped in expectation of my arrival, or whether they have *scattered* off and married, or what they may, can, must, might, could, would or should have done, I never ascertained. I got *out* of that scrape by *leaking out*, without using any great mixture of cunning, artfulness or ingenuity.

CHAPTER SIXTH.

The Author slopes—lucubrates—peforms some military manœuvres on the affections of his "antique relative," and legibilitates largely.

Soon after the incident recited in the last chapter, my term of school expired, and having bade adieu to friends and comrades, I set my face towards home. As I passed by the residence of Mr. Goodlesberry, my feelings were of a very peculiar and melting character. There was the yard in which Ellen and I had so often culled and exchanged pledges of constancy; there was the parlor from which I had so frequently heard the music of her sweet voice and the loud ring of her merry laugh; there, too, (on the shady side of this reverie,) was the spot where my matrimonial hopes had been "born, exhaled," and sent a scooting. I was leaving these scenes (now presenting the appearance of an impressive pantomime) to return perhaps no more forever. I felt gloomy and sad—none of your plaintive, lovelorn, whimsical sadness ; none of the gloom that oozes out of the heart in streaks of moonshine, and splatters of poetic sentimentality. No! no! no! My emotions were of a very different quality. They were such as can only be adequately delineated by introducing once more an example taken from my friends of the "brute creation." It is a custom among cattle—a custom "whereof the memory of cattle runneth not to the contrary"—to assemble in large numbers around the spot where a cow has kicked her last bucket, and paw, and scrape, and bellow, in the most solemn and affecting manner, until their hoofs are worn, their feet tired, their lungs exhausted, and

their voices hoarse from the effects of their dismal obsequies.
I felt as I imagine those cattle feel on such occasions. Now,
I don't compare Miss Ellen with a cow, and particularly do
I refrain from comparing her to one that has kicked a bucket
or anything else. She was to me

> " A star that's fallen ;
> A dream that's passed away."

I yet loved her, and felt a local attachment for the place ;
and, doubtless, had my impulses possessed no other facilities
for egress than those of the kine creation, I too might have
pawed, scraped and put up a very respectable one-horse
bellow.

After wasting the best part of a week in tedious and
wearisome travel, I arrived at the Huggins' House, where I
found Uncle Tim confined to his room by a mild attack of
rheumatism, gout or some other drawing-up ailment, which
drew upon me a pretty frigid reception. When I entered
the house, he was reading his Bible, or probably Mercer's
Cluster; he reached out his hand, told me " howdy," and
having turned up the whites of his eyes so as to glance at
me over the banister of his spectacles, asked me, " Where's
your wife ?" and without waiting for an answer, quietly
resumed his reading. I now brought the whole force of my
adroitness, audacity, mendacity and pertinacity to play upon
the fortress of his gullibility and kind-heartedness, which for
a while seemed ineffectual ; but having received timely reinforcements from the strongly garrisoned cerebellum of my
aunty, his obstinacy finally surrendered at discretion, and I
" found favor in his sight."

I had brought home with me a quantity of novels, and for
three months after my arrival I gave to them the sum total
of my time and attention. The consequence was, I became
thoroughly convinced that I had made a most egregious
faux pas in my previous matrimonial *coup de etat*. I believed when I met the woman assigned to me in the allot-
ments of Fate, I would experience a sort of electro-magnetic
feeling—a kind of unexplainable consciousness of the work-
ings of some mysterious invisible agency ; I expected the
bristles of my perceptive faculties would rise in an instant,

and the whole troop of my affections (like a gang of scared sheep) strike off at a two-forty rate in the direction of her ladyship; I thought the whole arrangement of love, court- ship and marriage would be a regular thorough-bred, syste- matical irresistibility. I believed, therefore, that had I married Ellen, I would have been playing a prank upon the regulations of "Manifest Destiny." I no longer held *her* responsible for my capsizion, nor found fault with her taste. She wasn't a free agent. How *could* I censure her, when I believed the "*nascitur not fit*" applied as well to wives as poets? No, indeed; I was glad of it. Upon reflection, she didn't suit me, any way; her nose was not "cut down, hewed out, surveyed and manufactured" like those I'd read of; her voice wasn't so overly "low and sweet," and her eye didn't possess the "Alonzo and Melissa" twinkle. In fact, she lacked lots of being up to the measure of perfection "nominated" in the books. Now, at the present writing, I am free to admit, that had some beneficent Genii secured me at that time a personal interview and audience with Miss Ellen, and had she smiled encouragingly upon me, all these captious objections would have melted like frost upon a house on fire.

In May or June of '33, my uncle bargained for a lot of land joining his farm, armed me with the "spondulics," mounted me on Jerusalem, his sway-backed pony, and sent me to Thomasville to pay over the money and receive the titles. Never was there exhibited a better specimen of Dr. Valentine on his "tour in search of the picturesque," since that gentleman alighted from his bellowsed steed, than I presented as I vaulted into my saddle and stuck spur to the said Jerusalem. But I won't *dwell* on this *discriptio per- sonæ*. No, I *won't* dwell on that *pint ;* indeed, were dwel- lings "as plenty as blackberries," I wouldn't dwell on a matter so personal and embarrassing.

Jerusalem seemed to be in a brown study the whole way, for which reason we were four days on the road, and during that time I didn't court, mentally, less than three hundred and twenty-seven times. I was, of course, accepted every pass, and got married without any very severe preliminaries.

On my arrival at Thomasville, I learned the gentleman I had come to see was not at home ; so I left the money to be paid over—left it with a fellow I had never seen nor heard tell of; gave him instructions to deliver it, have the deed executed and mail it to my uncle. After dispatching these dry business matters, I settled my bill, bestrode my nag, and made tracks for Dooly.

About ten or twelve miles from Thomasville, I fell in with Tom Perry, an old chum and school-fellow, who informed me his father resided in that neighborhood, and prevailed on me to halt and spend a few days with him. He was then *en route* for a barbecue, whither I consented to accompany him, and soon reached the place. A large crowd (for those days) was assembled ; much excitement prevailed, and expectation was on tiptoe to hear some blustering speeches. I took no interest in these matters, and am consequently unable to give any account of them. Tom introduced me to several jolly, nice lads, in compliment to whom, and in honor of which, I proceeded to soak my inner carcass with a thundering big drink. In process of time, dinner was announced, and we repaired to the table, where we found a

Barbecue that looked delicious;
Barbecue that smelt the same way ;
Barbecue that tasted ditto,
Fixed expressly to pitch into ;
Fixed for folks and fixed for people
Of all parties to pitch into ;
Such as Mister Pluri-bustah
Never eat nor never tasted.

For a season the stampede of viands was such, that the said viands might appropriately have sung the words of that familiar old song—

"Farewell, vain world, I am going home."

Now, stick a peg right here, until I finish a momentary digression.

In observing learnedly, that " a man always chooses to be present when his own face is being shaved," Tristram Shandy proceeds, with beautiful connectedness, to compliment the person who invented sleep. " In humble imitation of his august example," I hereby pledge myself to be one of

ten men to erect a monumental sand-hill over the last rest
ing place of that philanthropic individual who first discovered
the art of eating—for which purpose, I hereby set apart the
net profits arising from the sale of my pamphlet for the first
" forty days and forty nights" after its advent into this
" breathing world." I approve of eating. I could take
the stump in its advocacy. It is a subject upon which I am
a unit. But to my story :

I had not long been luxuriating in the masticatory amusements, (excuse splurging; by-the-way, I once had a pro-
tracted spell of the splurges, which finally assumed a chronic
type, and threatened me with very severe consequences : but
I am now well of it ;) I had not, I say, been long eating, when
I espied nearest to me, and across a corner of the table, one
of the most perfect beauties it has ever been my lot to aim a
pair of winkers at.

Talk about your " raven tresses hanging beside swan-like
necks ;" your " foreheads reposing in a bed of curls ;" your
" features cast in beauty's mould ;" your " eyes looking love
on eyes," &c ; all these were not a circumstance (at least not
one of the kind that alters cases) to the visible attributes of
my *incog*. neighbor, according to my then existing concep-
tions. Oh, what a sweet expression was there, my country-
men ! What beautifully chiselled lips (between which she
was engorging a huge fragment of a departed swine !) How
"fearfully and wonderfully" made ! I, of course, expe-
rienced the sensations 1 have been referring to. I felt as
plainly as I would have felt the jolt of a double-barrelled
earthquake, that she was to be mine.

At length she looked at me ; I saw a suppressed and bashful smile steal like a gleam of sunshine over the cerulean of
her countenance. Her glance produced a jerking sensation
in the region of my heart; I believed "Old Cubic had shot
her with his dart," as well as myself, and that nothing remained to be done but the performance of the usual ceremo-
nies. Again she bent on me her languishing eyes with such
a soft, bewitching fondness, that to have longer doubted the
mutuality of our love, would have caused a blush to mantle
on the cheek of outright skepticism. I determined to de-

mand an introduction forthwith. On looking around, however, I found my friend and new acquaintances were off on
a tramp, and couldn't be found; but I didn't whittle away
much time in coming to a conclusion as to what course I
would pursue in this emergency (if you prefer the expression); I didn't remain in the huckleberry-pond of doubt, so
that the waters of irresolution could make permanent rings
around the legs of determination. Not I; I had no idea of
acting the foolishly formal part of that individual, especially
notorious, who felt a delicacy in throwing a rope to a drown-
ing fellow-creature, unless he could first receive an introduction. No! no! I made up my mind to scare up a chat with
her. What subject I would first broach, and how I would
finally give a tongue to my "internal suggestions?" were
vexed questions, about which I was meditating when the
thread of my reflections was clipped by a movement on the
part of some of the ladies to leave the table. But there
stood my fair enchantress. Although she had finished eating,
she was still and motionless as " a painted ship on a painted
ocean "—riveted, no doubt, to the spot by a spell she wot not
of. " Poor creature," thought I, "it would be cruel to
sport longer with her affections by keeping her in suspense."
I accordingly sauntered a little nearer, and informed her I
had a question to ask. Of course, I didn't mean to ask *the*
question. I was going to suggest that she favored Miss
Ellen, and ask if they were related. When I spoke, three
different women (all old and ugly) thought I was looking at,
and speaking to, them, and each expressed themselves
" ready for the question." I apprised them of their mistake ;
but a woman's a woman, and they determined to witness all
the balance of my acts and doings on that occasion. My
purpose, however, was fixed. I attracted the young lady's
attention, and according to the programme laid down, again
reminded her I had a question to ask. She looked at me
with another of those sweet smiles, and after a silence of
about one minute—oh, how I hungered and thirsted to hear
the rich music of that voice! how I braced myself to bear
with equanimity its melting melody!—after a silence of
about one minute, during all of which time she looked at me
steadily with a soft, sweet smile, she remarked, in a tin-pan-

ish voice : " Ax on, hoss !" I've read of killing frosts, but this was a six-feet snow to my romantic, novel-engendered notions. My electro-magnetism for the time melted into " thin air." But I was committed to ask a question ; so, as soon as I recovered from the shock occasioned by her unexpected reply, I determined to gratify my curiosity on the subject of her strange demeanor. So I continued—" Why did you look at me so intently, and with such apparent concern, during dinner ?" " Bekase," said she, speaking with vim and feeling, " you wus so tarnashun ugly, I couldn't help it ; now you've got it !" Whereupon, she eyed me with scornful obliquity, and turned away. I looked around to see if any acquaintance had heard, or if anybody else had noticed this demonstration, and believing they had not, I sneaked away and soon fell in with Tom, and we sought the residence of the elder Perry. We had not been at home (Tom's home) long before my beauty passed by on foot, toteing her shoes in her hand ; and I learned she had actually walked nine miles to patronise the barbecue !

The sickness of my horse detained me with my friend Tom nearly a week. Fortunately, on my arrival at home, I found the deed had been executed and mailed, and had out-traveled me, and Uncle Tim was in fine spirits.

CHAPTER SEVENTH.

The Author enjoys the luxury of reciprocated affection, and receives a practical hint as to the course of true love.

I was now nearing my nineteenth birth-day, and didn't feel that I could, consistently with my inclinations, my sense of duty, and my responsibility as a gentleman and a member of society, longer defer committing the crime of matrimony. I grew anxious, restless and impatient on the subject. But I was surrounded by very considerable disadvantages. I lived in a neighborhood where a young lady's fascinations were determined by the number of lightwood-knots she could tote, or the facility with which she could balance a pail of

water on her head, while carrying a bucketful in each hand.
For these elegant and fashionable accomplishments I had no
particular relish, and was, therefore, ill at ease in my situation.   After a season, however, I formed the acquaintance of
Miss Betsy Barron—daughter of a wealthy farmer living
about twelve miles off—with whom I again determined to
put my sparking skill to the test.   She didn't fill the measure of my exacting and scrupulous taste, but she was a very
fair substitute ; quite a respectable make-shift ; the best I
could get under the circumstances.   And then, my uncle
had begun to lecture me seriously about leading an idle and
profligate life, and was anxious to aid in getting me employment in town.   I didn't want ·employment ; so, while I was
not mercenary, the hope of being in a situation above the
necessity of labor was quite an argument in answer to Miss
Betsy's short-comings. Every Sabbath that there was preach-
ing at the church in her father's neighborhood, I was in at-
tendance, rode home with her, and talked of love, poetry and
flowers, until, at length, I addressed her, and she consented
to marry me.   Yes, she actually fell in love with " me, even
me," and promised in good faith to be mine.   During my
next visit, I was to have a talk with the old folks, and in the
meantime she agreed to break the subject to them, that they
might have time for reflection.

Now, marriage began to stare me in the face as it had
never done before, and I set to reflecting in good earnest on
the difficulties my change of situation would produce. I had
never owned a darkey in all the days of my life ; had never
whipped, clothed nor allowanced one ; had never noticed
how many rows they could weed in a day ; didn't know
whether one or five hundred rails, boards or shingles would
be a task, and, in fact, had as little idea of domestic economy
as the antedeluvian world had of the ornamental elegance of
crinolizing.   A portion of these difficulties were removed in
the course of a conversation with Uncle Tim ; but the whipping—that was the matter that gave me pause. To be compelled to chastise a slave in the presence of my new wife, and
to perform that duty " so lamely and unfashionable," that she
would see poverty sticking out in the motion of my muscles,
and hear it in every crack of the whip, was a source of great

prospective embarrassment. Accordingly, I cut a long hickory switch, walked some distance in the woods, boldly confronted a huge pine tree, and set in as follows: "You haven't half worked, you good-for-nothing, trifling, contemptible, ungentlemanly, insignificant and villainous vagabond." Whereupon, I larrapped the tree most furiously. "Oh! pray, master!" said the imaginary negro—and I bungled awfully in trying to talk like a negro in distress. "Oh, yes," I continued, "you cherished the fond hope that I would not detect you; you vainly supposed you'd escape the punishment due to your infamous faithlessness," (talking; of course, for the ear of my wife, who was supposed to be present); and again did the uplifted blow descend with violence, and once more did the imaginary negro beg for dear life. The abuse, whipping and begging continued for about the space of twenty minutes, when, satisfied with the manner in which I had acquitted myself, I left off. Here I pause to correct an error in the traditions of those times. The report was then circulated, and is still believed by some, that Miss Betsy's brother was standing for a deer in fifty yards of the tree referred to, and heard all that passed. It is further believed, that in speaking to my supposed negro, I mentioned that I didn't marry his Miss Betsy to support her negroes in idleness—by which unfortunate observation, the rumor further states, I was foiled in endeavoring to form an alliance "offensive and defensive" with the Barron family. This report was unfounded and wholly incorrect. I admit, a man did occupy the stand hard by—perhaps a hundred yards off—and that he must have heard what passed; but he was no brother of Miss Betsy. As soon as I discovered him, I stationed myself behind a clump of bushes, and watched for fifteen minutes in the vain endeavor to ascertain who he was. If he ever related the circumstance, therefore, I am sure he didn't know who to tell on. I mentioned it confidentially to a number of friends afterwards, but I am certain that it never reached Miss Betsy's ears, at least, until after "the fitful dream was over." On the appointed Sabbath I saddled Jerusalem, and repaired to the church. I waited impatiently until a long-winded sermon was preached (strangely enough) from the text, "Ask and ye shall receive." Owing to the sickness of two negroes, none of the Barrons were in attend-

ance ; so, as soon as the benediction was pronounced, I cantered off to Maj. B.'s, where I met a warm and flattering
reception ; but the Major would persist in calling me " Bud "
and " Sonny," and after a while actually suggested that I
" go to play with little Johnny."

This observation not only convinced me that my corpus
wasn't in great demand among the family, but completely
put to rout my patience and all the gentler elements of my
nature.   I had regarded it rather in the light of a conde-
scension for me to marry Miss Betsy, and entertained no
doubt that the family would be highly elated at the idea of
an accession so desirable.   What, then, oh, reader, must have
been my feelings, on finding that they not only refused to
favor my suit, but actually treated my pretensions with gross
disrespect !

I assumed an air of inflexible sternness, looked as fiercely
as possible at the old gentleman, and addressed him as follows :   " Sir, your conduct on this occasion is destitute of a
parallel, and certainly without the semblance of a pretext."
" Do you reckon?" he interposed.   " I come, sir, to pay
your family a compliment ; to perform a grave and important duty ; to offer to your lovely daughter protection from

'The storms which we feel in this cold world.'

I come to ask her hand in marriage, but I find the prize I
desire to obtain is guarded (I had like to have said) by a
Python."   Giving me a growling, snarlish smile, he replied :
" And spozen you had a sed it, who'd a kern?"   " But no,
sir," I continued, " I respect you, and will ever treat you
with that consideration which is dictated by an ardent affection for your daughter."   " I shall be monstrous proud of
that," he observed.   " And, sir," said I, " in view of all the
circumstances, I demand an explanation of your very remarkable and extraordinary conduct."   " You-u-u do?" he
replied, (drawling out the latter part of the word "you," and
giving also a heavy accent to the "do.")   There was no use
of " multiplying words."   I didn't wait to hear more.   Oh,
how I would have rejoiced just then for the privilege of
treating him as I had treated his imaginary nigger.   On my

way to the gate I met Miss Betsy, who was weeping bitterly; but she dried up her tears, and we arranged preliminaries for a runaway scrape. The next Wednesday night was the time appointed. She was to entrust her baggage to a faithful servant, and take a seat beside me on horseback to the nearest Squire's, where we were to marry in hot haste. As I rode up to the gate, she was to hang out a signal, if all was right, and her parting injunction was, that if our plans were frustrated, I must escape unidentified, or all future prospects of a union would be defeated. Matters being thus arranged, we separated.

As I jogged leisurely homewards, I talked kind and piteously to Jerusalem about our empty stomachs and general companionship in troubles. I promised that, as a reward for his fidelity, his Miss Betsy's soft hand should at some future day roach his dishevelled mane, and that his declining years should be crowned with all the comforts and luxuries that earth could bestow. To which he only replied by occasionally elevating his ears and anon switching his tail. At length this *exparte* conversation was interrupted by the recollection that my uncle would be using his horses on the day stipulated, and that I didn't know where else I could borrow one, particularly since no person was permitted to know the urgency of the demand. I spent two days, however, scouring the neighborhood in search of the desired beast, and was at last driven to the necessity of procuring my friend Bill Weaver's donkey, which, to do him justice, was very gentle and warranted to tote twice. Thus fitted out, on Wednesday evening, at sunset, my long-eared quadruped bore me away. About midnight I rode up in front of Maj. B.'s residence and halted. Betsy hung out the signal, and I leisurely awaited her arrival. Just as she blew out her candle to come down stairs, my donkey raised an uproarous and boisterous bray, which set a whole caravan of dogs to barking (the donkey got bark) and running over each other in trying which could soonest reach us (the donkey and me.) It so happened, that on the Sunday night previous, an attempt had been made to break open the Major's smoke-house—since which time he had slept with one eye open, as the saying is. When, therefore, this braying and barking band struck up their serenade, he rushed out with such velocity, as to discompose everything except my animal and his dogs. Betsy, it seemed, was undiscovered, and, true to instructions, I endeavored to escape without detection. Donkey took the negative side of that question, and my motion, as well as myself, *wasn't* carried.

The donkey turned out to be spur-proof. The dogs and the Major came up; the former began to bite me and my gallant steed (without respect to persons); the latter to ask a great many unnecessary questions (at least they seemed so to me) about my name and business, while Sir Donkey, desiring to take part in the amusements of the occasion, commenced using his heels as though he were playing a specially interesting game of ball. In this crowded and embarrassed situation, I was literally compelled to carry on a hurried, triangular and disconnected conversation, which ran substantially thus:

"How do you do, Major—wo-oo-oo-o—it's me—begone—your dogs are—begone—your dogs are—be off—very severe, Major—going visiting—oh, Major, my dear sir—be done—wo-ooo—your dogs are—let go—biting me—going visiting—wo—let go." " Purty time o' night to be visitin'," said he. " Wo—hold still—be done—to see a sick man." " Wonder who he is; jest know he'll git well as soon as you git thar," he remarked, still holding both arms akimbo, and propping himself against a panel of the fence, quietly seeing his all-devouring dogs prey like vultures upon every accessible point of my defenceless carcass. " Reckon I won't cure him—wo—behave—you quit—if I—wo—don't get there—if I—wo—get eat up by—" At this moment I discovered myself lying all in a lump on the ground, and the dogs swarming around me, as though I had been a particularly palatable collation. One liked the drum-stick, and governed himself accordingly; another was fond of breast; another preferred a rib; another concluded he would take a bit of shoulder; and so on. One would begin to bite at a particular point, and not relishing the flavor of the diet, or finding the meat a little tough, would let go and set in somewhere else. Meanwhile the Major had begun to command the peace and suppress the row, by using the authority vested in him.

Finding my body dogless, I at length arose from the ground, with mouth and eyes full of sand, and half a score of wounds bleeding freely. But I had not time to fairly shake myself, when I felt the Major's foot, (he had concluded to bring up the unfinished business) driven at me with great force, and in kicks of alarming frequency. Believing I would have to come to it anyhow, I resumed my horizontal position in the sand, where I made up my mind to remain until the show was over. The Major, however, soon lifted me up, and after calling me "a dirt-eatin' cus," and several other very musical pet names, gave me a farewell kick, bade me to "leak out;" asked me when I'd "be 'round gal stealin' agin?" and desired my opinion as to whether the "course of true love" ran smooth, &c.

I didn't swap compliments with him, but mounting my donkey, (which, since the cessation of hostilities, had doubt less been all the time reflecting on the subject, and finally got his own consent to travel,) I "departed in peace," and reached home about broad daylight. I told my whole story from beginning to end to Uncle Tim and Aunt Jerushy. The former abused me violently, but threatened terrible vengeance upon the Major, and having eaten his breakfast, saddled his horse, and forthwith repaired to the seat of war. I had always regarded my uncle as a very dangerous and desperate man, and now I could not help shuddering for the fate of the Major. I believed that what little life he might have stowed away in his body after Uncle Tim got through with him, would be attributable to unmerited elemency. And I will do my uncle the justice to say that he would certainly have wreaked the threatened vengeance, but for the accident of the Major's happening to be a little too heavy for him. So, after receiving a severe pommelling, and being badly gnawed by the aforesaid dogs, my "antique relative" concluded *not to whip* the Major. I cannot here insert the particulars of this engagement; the reader may look for them when I construct my book of Military Tactics.

Uncle Tim reached home bruised, bloody and mad. I was the first person he encountered, and he feathered in on me so violently, I had to seek safety by hunting a "lodge" in the "vast wilderness" near by. There I remained for hours, debating the question: " Whether war, pestilence and famine are a circumstance to the troubles, dangers, disasters and ' Ups and Downs' of wife-hunting?"

CHAPTER EIGHTH.

The Author finds the plot of his fate thickening, and flies to physic for succor.

My troubles began now to multiply. In addition to the misfortunes I had met with, in the world of gallantry, my uncle was becoming very anxious for me to get employment ; again proposed to render me any aid in his power, and increased the number and frequency of his lectures, never failing to wind up by reminding me that I was " like a hog that eats his acorn without ever looking up to see where it comes from."

After holding a long, friendly interview with myself, I finally concluded to study physic, and without any consultation or advice from anybody, I pitched into Gunn's Domestic Medicine, which I read and re-read, until I was completely master of its contents ; then, in order to give myself a little professional prestige, I regarded a short absence from home necessary, and accordingly spent the whole month of May (1834) with my friend Tom Perry, of Thomas—during which time I hunted, fished, &c., never looking between the lids of a book. On my return home, I made the startling announcement that I was a new-fledged Doctor, and stuck up notices on at least twenty-five trees, to the effect that I would repair worn-out constitutions on the shortest notice, and administer healing balms after the newest and most approved style.

My books were Gunn's Domestic Medicine, the Family Physician and Gregory's Elements: my medicine consisted of several phials of Bateman's Drops, Laudanum and Paregoric, four bottles of Rowan's Tonic, some Calomel, Quinine, Peruvian Bark and Salts. To be restricted to these anodynes was embarrassing. I believed there was something in a name, and I wanted a medicine with which neighbors and patients would not be so familiar, and by possessing which I hoped to secure to my professional claims respect and confidence. Uncle Tim, finding I had a mind to be at something, generously proffered to assist me, and actually advanced twenty-five dollars to be appropriated to the purchase of physic. I forwarded the money to Savannah with instructions to let me have the worth of it in medicines that couldn't kill ; to send, also, a catalogue of diseases they would cure, and the quantity to administer, and to be certain and label each and all with loftiest possible technicality. In the meantime, I began to get practice. I knew nothing about temperaments, regulating doses according to the violence of the disease, nor could I tell, except in extraordinary cases, whether the system was right, wrong, or in a state of betweenity. Indeed, I was never more ignorant, practically and theoretically, on any subject, than that which I now professed to have mastered. But I didn't believe I could go far wrong while I followed Gunn. I never studied about whether a disease was in a primary, secondary, or tertiary stage. My only inquiry was, How much was a dose for adults, and how much for children ? and I physicked according as the patient belonged to the one or the other class. My plan for finding out whether a patient was dangerous was to ascertain if the family were uneasy about his recovery. If they were, I felt his pulse, asked one or two questions in a concerned manner, and buried myself in a deep study, during which I took occasion to shake my head in a very doleful and significant way. Now, all this time the family were all attention, looking at the Doctor, and giving to every motion of his *finger* an important meaning. At length, perhaps, some old lady—not satisfied with the diagnosis of a better posted, but less pretentious, individual—would ask me, " What's his ailment ?" Of course, I had too much prudence at such times to venture an intelligible reply, at the risk of running foul of the experience of some person perfectly familiar with the symptoms; so I'd answer, " It's an enlargement, ma'am, of the ultimate corpustles of the pericardium." " Hit's what you mout call bilious fever, ain't it, Doctor ?" a modest individual would observe. Scarcely waiting to give an affirmative reply, my custom was to hunt

up Guun's prescription for bilious fever, which being administered, I was almost certain to effect a cure and gain professional character thereby. I cite this as an example of the
mode in which I was wont to hobble along in my profession.
I had always a number of set phrases with which to mystify
and becloud my ignorance, but none of the various expedi-
ents I resorted to came up in every instance to the full
measure of their commission. I was once called to the house
of a widow lady, whose only child was sick. All widows so
circumstanced are uneasy, and I was thus deprived of any
means of learning the severity of the disease, nor could I
tell with more than ordinary guess-work what disease it was.
I was, indeed, in a great strait. I could physic for fever,
and certainly a patient who has no fever is never much in
danger. But this wouldn't do ; I had too much conscience
to tamper with human life. " Now," thought I, " I can call
Dr. Smith in consultation, but this will probably expose my
ignorance in very distressing prominence to that known and
skillful practitioner (who subsequently told me, in confidence,
he had read exactly the same course I had.) Dr. Smith
may decide that it is nothing but a mild type of tertiary
headache, and then I will be ruined." At the conclusion of
this soliloquy, which brought large drops of perspiration to
my face, I found that the widow, who had twice asked me
about her child without receiving an answer, was indulging
in a small-sized cry. I determined to relieve her at the risk
of consequences, and immediately observed : " Mrs. Morgan,
you needn't be uneasy ; I'll soon cure him ; the disease is
nothing more than a flatulent suppuration of the vascular
thorax." At this the old lady quit crying, and I was again
bewildered by a multitude of meditations. After a while I
determined to call in Dr. Smith anyhow, and turned to give
instructions to that effect, when I saw Ben Herring walk in
at the gate. Oh, reader, what a salvo was his presence to
my wounded pride! I knew that he had had considerable
sickness in his family, and that if ever there was one individual on earth prouder of displaying his knowledge than all
the balance, Herring was that individual. He walked into
the room, spoke to the widow and myself, sidled up to the
bed of h e patient, looked at his tongue, felt his pulse and—
during Mrs. Morgan's temporary absence from the room—

observed: "Ain't much the matter, Doctor; hit's only got a lite fever thrum eatin' a *leetle* too much dirt." To this unsolicited observation I gave a knowing nod, and soon after began to administer the antidote in such cases made and provided, and by which I effected a speedy cure, and gained the confidence and friendship of the family.

About this period—that is to say, the first of September, 1834—my box of medicines arrived, and was stowed away in my room on shelves erected for the purpose. The labels read thus: Aquaticum, Carthamus Tinctorius, Linaria Vulgaris, Triticum Repens, Robinia Pseudocacea, Phytolaca Decandria, Podophyllum Pelatena, and Oil Tiglium, which last potation, it is said, Dr. Slawkinbergius once administered to a patient in doses of fifteen drops every fifteen minutes for fifteen days. With the medicines I received a letter, assuring me they were all mild and innocent, and enclosing a printed statement of their qualities and ingredients, which statement, being couched in technicalities, I threw in the fire. Finding I had one empty bottle, I levied light contributions from each of my preparations, and made a mixture, to which I gave the name of Bum Squintum, which I stated to inquirers would only cure when all other medicines failed. This announcement gave the word quite a currency in that section. A man, in charging another with being a liar, or a great rascal, was sure to observe, that "nothin' but Bum Squintum would koar his karrector." The love-sick swain could not successfully let off the exuberance of his feelings without remarking, "That gal is in the last stages of purtiness; she needs Bum Squintum." If a fond mother desired to chide her darling boy for rudeness, she threatened him with a dose of Bum Squintum, which invariably silenced the turbulent Bobby, and so on to the end of the chapter. I soon embarked in a flourishing practice, which served to increase the number of my embarrassments, and render me still more heartily tired of a profession for which I was so little qualified.

I regret that I have not space to insert a few more scraps of my experience as a Doctor, but a sense of duty admonishes me to hasten on. A circumstance occurred about the first of December, which " hauled me up with a short jerk in the middle of my kurreer."

Some workmen were repairing a house for my uncle, when one of them had his shoulder dislocated by a fall. I was, of course, called in to set the bone. I didn't know whether to push, pull or twist, and in making the poor, suffering mortal think I was administering to his relief, I bungled so awkwardly, that another workman discovered my ignorance, and came down, performed the operation, and very knowingly instructed me in the mysteries of bone-setting. This was the *coup de grace* of my professional life. Without more ado, I astonished everybody (myself included) by throwing physic to the dogs, and declaring I was willing, able and ready to whip every person who should ever in future take the liberty to dub me Doctor.

Having collected up and shaved off all the debts due me for services rendered, I borrowed the immortal Jerusalem, and on the 20th of December, set out for Athens, professedly in search of employment, but really on a wife-hunting and doctorship-avoiding expedition.

CHAPTER NINTH.

Tac Author again yields to the benign influence of woman—surrenders at discretion, but is not overly discreet in surrendering.

Uncle Tim's oldest son (Aminidab) and family resided in Macon, and with them I determined to spend Christmas, and endeavor to widen the circle of my female acquaintances.

Here, oh, generous and humane reader, " my heart grows sad as I ponder " on the mournful sequel of this visit. Memories of the past crowd thickly and heavily upon me, and now, late in the evening of my days, I feel a gloomy, heart-sickening realization, that

I never loved a dear young belle,
　To glad me with her soft black eye,
But when she came to know me well,
　She'd kick me (so to speak) sky-high.
I never loved a darling critter,
But some one else was sure to git her;
I never courted nary she,
But answered spatly "No-sir-ee!"

But I have no time to linger by the wayside. On the second day after my arrival in Macon, I formed the acquaintance of Miss Julia Wilkes, the most palpable and unmitigated specimen of a coquette that has existed within the memory of the oldest inhabitant. She certainly must have graduated, and taken the first honor at a flirting school. She was handsome, graceful and fluent, and free and easy in her deportment. Before the first evening of our acquaintance had passed, she fingered every string in the harp of my gullibility (if you will allow the metaphor.) She said, "at *first*, she was struck with my personal appearance (no doubt she was); had strange feelings towards me which she could not explain, or account for; didn't think I fancied her; was afraid I wouldn't relish her familiarity; couldn't act otherwise than she did; to be a woman was to be weak, susceptible and candid, and these were the elements in her character to which her conduct was attributable," &c. It taxes credulity to believe that ever a mortal was imposed upon by this transparent insincerity; but such was my lot, and I can prove it, if necessary. When she mentioned her "strange feelings," my belief in matrimonial fatality revived. I thought I felt in good earnest the premonitory symptoms of matrimony, and mentally, as was my custom, ran ahead and arranged everything but the practical results. I reflected on what time we should appoint to marry; who we would invite from Dooly; how Uncle Tim and aunty would treat her kindly and let her have her own way, after they got done fussing; how she and I would stroll by moonlight, and luxuriate forever in the extacies of a perennial honey moon, (gracious! ain't the dictionary words holding a "big meeting?") and never grow old in feeling, nor troubled by cares.

I called to see her on the next night, and the third, and during all this time she did *so* much to increase my affection; sung so many plaintive songs—to which my heart, of course, played suitable accompaniments—and made such pretty, winning remarks, that on my fourth visit I proposed and she accepted me. "Don't consult my parents yet," said she; "let's not be in too great a hurry; we have, at best, but a short time to be young, and mingle in society, for after marriage we will, to a great extent, be shut out and excluded from the world. I am certain nothing can change my feelings or cool the ardor of my affection for you. Return to your rural home, and come again in the early part of the Spring, and I will covenant at the altar to go with you on to the end, till a shadowy hand shall separate us at the grave. But you must write to me frequently. I am sure I shall shed tears if you don't." I approved the suggestion, and would have approved any she might have made, and promised to write to her often. I told her I would leave for Athens on the morrow, and call to see her as I returned; after which, we shook hands feelingly and separated.

Accordingly, after dinner the next day, I set out for old Clarke. A mile from Macon I was overtaken by a fellow-traveler, who was going my road about forty miles. He was a stout, brawny young man, a little to the starry side of six feet high, wore coarse, number-ten brogan shoes, brown linen pants, and a linsey-woolsey roundabout coat, from the pocket of which a huge ginger-cake was "visible to the naked eye;" in fact, projecting "in an open manner, and fully exposed to view." He chewed tobacco as though he had a special spite at the weed, and spat by streaming the juice through his teeth with a dexterous flirt of the tongue.

We soon exchanged names, and I found him a companionable, clever fellow. I was fretted, though, at his continuing to call me "Mister" and "Stranger," after I had told him my name; but charging these trifling errors to the credit of his honest ignorance, I bore them patiently. He informed me he lived near Macon; was then on a pleasure trip, to take a *coup d'œil* (he didn't say so) of the world, and that his father had a good number of "black ones." At the conclusion of this epitome of his life, to show he wasn't stingy, if he was rich, he generously divided the cake with me, and reaching a hand into his saddle-bags, drew out another, which he deposited in a manner equally as conspicuous as the former.

Thus we traveled on, becoming better and better acquainted, and more and more friendly. At night we took a bed together, and both retired early: but, though wearied, my heart was in Macon, and I couldn't sleep. After rolling for about two hours, "chewing the cud of sweet and bitter fancies," I heard my bed-fellow clear his throat in such an intelligent manner, I knew he was awake. "Haven't you been asleep?" said I. "Not yit," he replied, and heaving a deep sigh, he turned over. "Have you ever been in a love scrape?" I asked, in a beseeching tone. "In one now," said he: "that's what ailds me." I informed him I was deprived of sleep by the same cause. "Ingaged to yourn?" he inquired. I told him I was. "Did you buss yourn's paw when you seed her last?" he continued. I informed him I had not enjoyed that luxury. "Then I am one on you, Mister," said he; and rejoicing in his advantage over me, he soon fell to snoring. I pictured to myself his rustic lassic—

"In simple peasant guise"—

using her untutored graces to win his love, and returning it with a fondness and sincerity that would admit of no counterfeit. I drew the parallel between her and the accomplished Julia, and in *my* turn, *rejoicing in the advantage I possessed* over him, soon fell asleep, dreamed, and *got even* with my bed-fellow by kissing Julia's hand. Betimes, next morning, we arose, breakfasted, and were moving "on our winding way." Of course, we soon began to swap secrets. Each loved the cleverest, prettiest, loveliest and most constant of her sex. I could never again cherish sentiments of affection for any other lady but *mine*, and he "couldn't never love nobody but *his'n*." Gradually we became more and more confidential, until at length, oh! startled reader, the fact broke in (burglariously) upon our minds, that we were both engaged to the same female whirligig! This discovery drew much redness and heavy drops of perspiration to the face of my friend, Dick Small, (I beg pardon for not introducing him by name when he first made his appearance,) and caused him to grind on his cud of tobacco with still more savage ferocity.

Just think about it: That mouth, from whose corners the juice was freely oozing, had actually imprinted a kiss on the fair hand of the charming Julia! The very suggestion sickened me. I (who had learned to bear misfortunes) held my

peace, but Richard waxed vociferous; "She was the out-
bangenest critter he had ever seed; had tuck sich pains to
tell him he was the likest youngster she knowed of; had said
so much about gwine with him to the grave, (a place he
never did keer much about going to,) and cackled at him
so many of them thar blasted pianner songs, and then, arter
all, she'd told him she'd marry him. But," said he, mod-
erating his voice, "I reckin maybe she's in *yearnest* about
me, and jest makin' sport outen *you*."

We agreed, on our return to Macon, to call to see her on
the same evening. We were to drop in as strangers, and
make such forcible and pointed references to our engage-
ments, as would compel Julia to "show her hand." We
both regarded her conduct highly censurable, and promised
to mortify and embarrass her to the extent, that that object
could be accomplished by these insinuations. I engaged to
show her no quarter, and *he* said *he* "wouldn't have no com-
parison on her." At length our roads diverged and we separated. The strange disclosures of the morning occupied
my thoughts for many miles, until, at last, I found comfort
in the firm conviction that my friend Dick was right; only
I believed *he* was the victim, and *I* the fortunate individual.

At Athens, I was welcomed by my old host, hostess and
many friends, who seemed glad to see me; said I had im-
proved wonderfully, and treated me as if I were a distin-
guished visitor. I wanted to enquire after Ellen, but I
couldn't. The word choked utterance, for even the children
of that generation were familiar with my courtship in the
Goodlesberry family.

A few days after my arrival, however, a number of ladies
and gentlemen paid a pop-call to my hostess, and among
them was my former idol. She met me very cordially, introduced me to the company, and taking a seat near me,
asked so many questions about my health, happiness and
prospects in life, and exhibited such earnest solicitude in my
behalf, that I *knew* in a moment she was now willing, anxious, to marry me. And, reader, when I inform you that
she looked young, fresh and ruddy, the very image of her
former self; that she talked as blandly, and smiled as sweet-

ly, as ever before, do you wonder that I became "gloriously reconciled" to her? Yes, I resolved to let Julia "rip," and remain in the neighborhood until I could arrange the grand finale of matrimony with lovely Ellen. After half an hour's busy chat with me and others, (during which time I was growing more and more furiously in love with her,) she arose to leave. Again giving me her hand warmly, she remarked: "You must be sure to call and see"—"Yes, ma'am, I will," said I, energetically interrupting her—" my baby." " Are you married?" I innocently asked, or rather gasped, while blushes swarmed like bees over my face. Her husband was the gentleman standing nearest me, and a fine, healthy-looking specimen he was. Seeing I was so deeply bewildered, he generously pulled me along, and I went and took supper at his house, saw the baby, and, in the main, spent rather a pleasant evening.

I made two or three ineffectual and rather sluggish efforts to get employment, and finally concluded to go home and study law. Accordingly, at the expiration of my allotted time amongst the scenes and with the companions of other days, I left, and reached Macon without accident, and in due season.

On the evening agreed upon by Dick Small and myself, I called to see Miss Julia, who I found busily engaged entertaining a fine, genteel, intelligent, handsome young man.— My arrival produced no very great commotion. She spoke to me with an air of easy familiarity; asked when I returned; siad she was happy to see me, and having introduced me to her friend, resumed her seat near him, and soon seemed wholly forgetful of my presence.

I felt sensibly that I was a " neglected genius." She was actually talking to her new victim much after the same manner she had conversed with me, and that, too, in my " personal presence." Now, I again warn the reader. that although this looks a little unreasonable, I am willing to make the proof, if any person should so far forget the civilities of society as to dispute my word.

At length honest Dick " arriv." He walked in as though the premises were " his'n," and evidently intending to convince me at the go-off upon what familiar terms he was with the fair resident, he went boldly up to her and said, "How-dy, July, old gal, how's yore feelins?" She repaid this fa-miliarity with such a freezing coolness, as disarmed even him. Having repaired to a convenient seat, he spent a half hour in silently listening to the lovers. Occasionally he would give me a glance, which seemed to say, "We ain't a gittin' even with her much," while as for myself, I honestly confess, I felt very much like a sheep-devouring member of the canine fraternity. At length we both arose to leave.— Miss Julia invited us to sit longer ; said it wasn't late, and declared she would "feel hurt" if we left so early. Where-upon, we resumed our seats, and she again sidled up to her dandy and lost sight of us.

Now, I didn't think I made a very handsome parlor orna-ment, and as my presence was serving, and likely to serve, no other purpose, I soon began to regret my folly in con-senting "not to hurt" Miss Julia's feelings by leaving. But to leave or not to leave, wasn't the question ; at least, it wasn't an open question, having been settled in a manner I was pledged to abide by.

I therefore made up my mind to "grin and bear it."— Dick, however, was not altogether so scrupulous in the ob-servance of commitals. He smashed his hat on his head violently, crammed both hands in the bottoms of his breech-es pockets, fiercely exclaiming, "By jucks, I'm a gwine," he made long, mad steps to the door, and passed out uninter-rupted. This furnished me a pretext for leaving, and in a few moments more I also departed. I found friend Dick sta-tioned at the gate, standing sentinel, armed with a terrible bludgeon, vehemently swearing that he "wouldn't leave none of that thar band-box man for the buzzards, agin he got through with him."

I do not intend here to state whether the gallant Richard executed this dreadful threat. Whether the said Richard actually "fotch him up a standin'," or [acting in obedience to the kindly impulses of a generous nature] had "compari-son" on the poor fellow, I refuse to tell. These matters come under the head of Military Tactics, and shall be em-braced in my work on that subject. I will not, "at present," say whether they fought, or even quarrelled ; but this I will observe, for the benefit of those who are shuddering for the fate of the band-box man : he lived and got over it.

FINIS.